BRENDA GAYLE

Seasons of Love - Winter

Six Geese for Monica
Seasons of Love - Winter
by Brenda Gayle
Published Internationally by Bowstring Books
Ottawa, Ontario, Canada

Previously published by The Wild Rose Press as *Six Geese for Monica*
(*Twelve Brides of Christmas Series*)
©2014 Brenda G Heald
Re-edited & re-published as *Six Geese for Monica (Seasons of Love - Winter)*
©2025 Brenda G Heald

EBOOK ISBN: 978-1-7387434-8-3
PRINT ISBN: 978-1-7387434-9-0
LARGE PRINT ISBN: 978-1-0695819-0-7

ONE

The white beast sprinted toward her, stopping only a few metres away before stamping its foot and hissing loudly.

The speed with which the bird moved and the raucous sounds it made brought a gasp from Monica Stevens.

Where the heck did that come from?

Keeping one eye on the attack guard, she cautiously angled her body to retrieve her suitcase from the back seat of the ridiculously tiny rental car. The attendant had assured her it was all they had available, but she was equally certain that what he really wanted was to get the ugly thing off his lot as quickly as possible. Given its shape and colour, it looked more like a wedge of cheese on wheels than a functioning automobile.

A whoosh of air whipped around her as the beast reared up, its broad wingspan making it triple in size. Abandoning the suitcase, she pressed back against the door of the vehicle. As the bird moved ever closer, its hissing was accompanied by a rhythmic thumping sound.

It was pure white, except for bright orange patches on its face and feet. And its eyes were a startling, brilliant blue—so very disconcerting.

Would staring at it be taken as a sign of aggression? A dog you'd avoid staring down, but what about a goose?

Monica lowered her gaze, just in case, and realized she was standing in a puddle of water left by melting snow. Her new burgundy pumps were now soaking wet.

Perfect.

Less than twenty-four hours ago she'd been sitting on her porch, at home on Vancouver Island, sipping a nice Chardonnay and watching the sun dip low over the Clayoquot Sound. Three flights, innumerable delays, and a horrendous two-and-a-quarter-hour drive from Ottawa, which should only have taken ninety-minutes but for the slush-covered roads, and Monica was back in Havenport, Ontario. From the majestic Pacific Ocean to dreary Big Rideau Lake in only fifteen hours; ironic how mere minutes can bridge a lifetime.

The goose took another menacing step closer.

Okay, she needed to do something. If she could open the car door, maybe she could sound the horn and scare it away. Or at the very least tap out an S-O-S to call for help.

She reached behind and felt for the door handle.

Slowly, don't antagonize the bird. Don't look at it. Look somewhere else. Over there, by the tree swing...

"Holy heck!" Monica froze when she spotted two pairs of brown eyes peering out at her from behind the giant oak tree. Now, what should she do? The kids couldn't be more than three or four years old. She had to make sure the beast didn't turn on them.

"Stay where you are." She tried to sound calm, not wanting to frighten the children or provoke the bird.

Two boys with straight, jet-black hair, dressed in matching yellow rain slickers and black rubber boots, emerged from behind the tree. Then, to her horror, they began walking toward her.

She had to do something. She'd read how vicious geese could be, and this bird was certainly living up to the reputation. Two little boys wouldn't stand a chance.

"No, stop! Don't move."

And of course, they didn't listen. They continued to approach her, giggles erupting from their throats. At any moment the goose would see them and…

"*Woa-ah-ee-ee!*" Monica hadn't known she was capable of making such an obnoxious sound, but she screamed it and lunged at the bird, flapping her arms in the air.

"What on earth? Monica? What are you doing?" a voice called from behind her.

The goose appeared mildly taken aback by Monica's performance. Then, after seeming to give her a disdainful glare, it turned and, half flying and half hopping, returned to wherever it had come from.

The boys had stopped dead in their tracks, staring at her, mouths open wide. Monica turned toward her sister who seemed equally astonished.

Sure, now you show up. "I had to stop it from going after the boys." Monica took a deep breath to slow her pounding heart. "What the heck is Mom th-thinking, having a g-g-goose like that with l-l-l-little k-k-k-kids?" She started shivering. Her sweater wasn't warm enough to keep away the bitter cold, and she'd lost the feeling of her toes. She'd forgotten that, in this part of the country, snow in October was common.

Cathy Jenning's eyes shone with humour as she engulfed Monica in a hug. "Welcome home, Sis."

Monica stepped back and ruefully returned the smile. Cathy had a way of taking the sting out of life. But then, she'd always gotten everything she'd wanted. Three years Monica's junior, her sister was married to a great guy, had two teenaged daughters, and loved her job as a teacher at the local elementary school. Monica envied her but didn't begrudge Cathy her happiness. "It's not my home, anymore."

"It is for the next two months, at least," Cathy said.

Monica eyed her suspiciously. "Don't get any ideas that I'm going to stay. I'm just here to help out while Mom recovers from her surgery. How is she? Have you heard how it went?"

"Yes, the hospital called a while ago. The hip replacement went fine. We can visit for a short time tonight, after supper."

"Good."

Their mother was strong and in incredibly good physical shape for a woman in her late sixties. Plus, she'd always been blessed with excellent health. Monica was optimistic that the two months the doctors anticipated would be required for Terry to fully recover was a worst-case scenario. With any luck, Monica would be back in temperate British Columbia before Christmas.

"He's a gander, by the way," Cathy said over her shoulder after Monica had retrieved her suitcase and was following her up the stairs onto the veranda. "Kristoff. His mate and their goslings were killed by coyotes last summer. He's been over-protective of the twins ever since. I think he's lonely."

"Kristoff?" Monica pushed away a stirring of sympathy for Kristoff the gander. "That's a pretty fancy name for a goose...I mean gander."

Cathy laughed. "Yes, after the iceman in *Frozen*." She paused. "You've heard of *Frozen*, right?"

"*Let it go*," Monica sang the popular refrain "I've never seen it, but that song is pretty hard to ignore."

"Well, trust me, you'll be well versed in all things Arendelle before you leave. Naming him Kristoff was Kate's idea. She's in that dreaming-of-prince-charming stage."

"Hmm, I'm not sure that's something to be encouraged," Monica muttered.

"What's that?"

Monica knew Cathy heard her, so she didn't bother repeating her comment and risk having the conversation divert into a direction she wasn't prepared to go. "I don't think geese are an appropriate choice to have around young children. How many does Mom have?"

"Five now. And they're easier than goats."

"*Five?* Why not a dog? Or why have anything at all? It's not like she doesn't already have enough to take care of with running a daycare full of kids," Monica persisted, easily falling into the familiar pattern of sibling bickering.

"Mother Goose Daycare should have geese," Cathy said, holding open the front door.

Before Monica could enter, two small bodies scurried past. "Boots off! Coats up!" Cathy and Monica called together, echoing their mother's familiar refrain to them when they were younger.

"Yup, it's good to have you back," Cathy said, giving Monica another hug.

Monica stood in the hallway and gasped. She was unprepared for the physical cinching of her gut in reaction to the emotional onslaught she experienced stepping back into her childhood home. It smelled just as she remembered—a combination of her mother's favourite lemon cleanser, hardwood polish, and sugar cookies. No doubt Mom had baked a batch, or twelve, in preparation for her absence—or of Monica's arrival. This particular recipe was Monica's favourite treat, and her mother had always had a fresh batch ready whenever she came home from an overnight sleepover or summer camp—even those first years of college.

It was as if nothing had changed in the big rambling farmhouse over the past seven years. The front hall was littered with boots and shoes of various sizes, an assortment of kid-sized fall and winter jackets hung from hooks on the wall. The big oak staircase stretched out to her left, leading to the five upstairs bedrooms.

The kitchen was at the end of the hallway. She heard the boys laughter over the scraping of a chair along the kitchen floor. They were after cookies, she was quite certain.

"We'd better get in there or who knows what kind of mess we'll find," Cathy said.

Monica followed her sister along the hallway, glancing to her right as they passed the front sitting room and *dining room?* She paused on the threshold and slowly entered what she remembered had been the formal dining area. Her mother's twelve-person mahogany table and chair set had been removed, replaced by a double bed and nightstand. A television sat on the buffet, surrounded by pictures of Monica and Cathy; their hazel eyes peering out from beneath a variety of dreadful hairstyles in a rainbow of colours. After moving to Vancouver Island, Monica had forsaken the blonde she'd adopted in her twenties and thirties to return to her natural brown.

"Mom moved down here a year ago," Cathy said from behind. "The stairs were getting to be too much."

"The dining set?" Monica said and then felt stupid.

"Phil and I have it, but if you want…" Cathy said and looked down, almost guiltily.

"No," Monica said quickly and brushed past her sister to continue into the kitchen. "That's not what I meant. Sorry."

She didn't know which she found more disconcerting —how many things had remained the same or how much had changed.

What did you expect?

The only thing she was sure of was that she had never expected to return to Havenport again.

"How about some tea?" Cathy asked.

"Got anything stronger?"

"Devon, Derrick, say 'hello' to Monica," Cathy said, ignoring Monica's half-joke. "She's going to be looking after you for a while. Monica is my sister and Nanny-Goose's daughter."

Nanny-Goose?

"Deal with it!" Cathy murmured, catching Monica's sardonic glance.

The two boys climbed down off the chair and solemnly shook Monica's hand. "I'm very pleased to meet you, Devon and Derrick," she said.

"What shall we call you?" one asked. Devon? Derrick? Presumably, she'd eventually figure out which was which.

"Sissy-Goose?" the other suggested.

Monica scowled at Cathy's snort of laughter. "How about Monica?" she said, turning back to the boys.

"That's boring," said Devon or Derrick, "but okay."

"Well, now that that's settled," Cathy said, "why don't you boys go meet the bus so you can introduce Monica to your brother and sisters while you all have a snack."

The boys hollered in glee and raced back to the front hall. There was a clamour of noise as they jumped to reach their coats and stamped into their boots before the door slammed shut, leaving the women in blessed silence.

"Twins?" Monica asked.

Cathy shrugged. "They're about the same age."

"So, tell me about this family and why they were the only ones you couldn't find an alternate daycare for while Mom is recuperating?"

"Luke McMillan is a great guy. He has six kids—"

"Six! How old?"

"Four of them are in school. Michael's nine, Kate is eight, Lucy is seven, and Ophelia is six. Devon and Derrick are the only ones you'll have for the full day. The others will come for an hour or two after school."

"Six children under the age of ten?"

"I couldn't find a daycare that could take all six, and Luke didn't want to separate them."

"Where's their mother?" Monica asked, still having difficulty envisioning a family with so many children who were so close in age.

"She died a year-and-a-half ago from a brain aneurism. It was very sudden and very tragic. She was a lovely woman. They were a lovely family. They moved here not long after you'd left, I think. Beth's death hit everyone pretty hard—especially the older kids."

Monica stared down at her hands. Even after seven years, she could still see the pale shiny indentation in her flesh made by her wedding band. She had come to terms with the end of her marriage and all that had led up to it. At the time, she'd thought her situation was tragic. But a young woman robbed of the chance to raise her children, to celebrate their birthdays, graduations, marriages, and to see her grandchildren? *That* was a real tragedy.

Monica raised her gaze to her sister's. "Life is so unfair, isn't it?"

Cathy reached out and squeezed Monica's hand. "Are you going to be okay with this?"

"I don't know, Cath. I hope so."

TWO

Luke McMillan glanced down at his watch. Six-ten. *Late again.*

He wrenched open the door to the minivan and threw his briefcase across the seat, sliding in after it. Thank goodness for Terry Stevens. If it wasn't for her, and her daughter Cathy's family, he'd be in a real bind. He cranked the engine and peeled out of the parking lot, cursing the spray of slush that splashed across the windshield. It was already dark. The kids would be anxious.

One of the things Luke loved about Havenport was the ability to get virtually anywhere within a couple of minutes. The town—that was a generous term—was really nothing more than a cluster of a half-dozen streets extending off of Highway 15 to the shore of Big Rideau Lake.

It was growing, though, now serving as a bedroom community for nearby Kingston and, for those more adventurous, the larger city of Ottawa. There were a few businesses: a gas station with a snack bar, a hardware store, a hairdresser—well, a woman who cut and coloured her customers' hair in her kitchen—a post office, and a municipal planning and development office.

It was an odd, out-of-the-way place to have a development office—no doubt someone owed someone a favour—but it suited Luke just fine. He was an architect, and it was conveniently close for meetings with planning officials, which is what he'd been doing all friggin' day. The amount of bureaucracy these small-town planners could dream up was mind-numbing. In the end, he'd gotten his way, as he knew he would—he just wished it hadn't taken nine hours for them to see reason. The local council *said* it wanted its community to grow in a way that took advantage of all the latest environmentally sustainable technologies. Since that was what he specialized in—and they'd hired him—you have thought they'd have been more agreeable to his proposal.

Luke pushed away his frustrations of the day and slowed his minivan to turn into the Stevens' driveway. The bright orange-coloured vehicle startled him. Terry must have a visitor. He hoped his tardiness hadn't interfered with her plans. Must be an out-of-towner. On these roads, you'd like something a little larger than a subcompact. He got out of his minivan and examined the car more closely. All-season tires? *Good luck in a month when the weather really turns nasty.* The rental sticker confirmed his first thought and he decided to cut the visitor some slack. They probably didn't know better and likely wouldn't be here longer than a few days.

He felt the vibration of his cell phone in his pocket

before the strains of "Let it Go" began. He retrieved it, glanced at the name *L. Burkholder*, closed his eyes, and sighed deeply. *Nope, not going to deal with her today.* He couldn't avoid her forever, but it was after six o'clock and he was on family time now. The fact she'd left three messages earlier in the day…? Well, he'd been busy, hadn't he? He declined the call and turned off his phone.

"Hello!" Luke called, opening the front door and bracing himself for the usual onslaught of enthusiastic hugs. There was a commotion in the kitchen and then an unfamiliar voice, but no children. He kicked off his boots to investigate.

He was greeted by a chorus of "Hello, Daddy" as he entered the kitchen, but his six children remained seated at the table, plates in front of them piled high with spaghetti. A woman he didn't recognize rose. "Mr. McMillan, I presume. The children were hungry waiting for you, so I prepared them dinner."

She was attractive with shoulder-length brown hair, a bright floral short-sleeve blouse with turquoise ankle-length pants—a little dressy for kids and spaghetti—and over-sized grey work socks on her feet. She had a warm sun-drenched glow to her skin, but her perfectly applied make-up couldn't hide the dark, puffy sign of fatigue around her eyes. Those eyes he recognized—just like her mother's and her sister's—however, their expression of displeasure was not something he was used to seeing from the Stevens women.

"Where is Terry?" he asked.

"Hospital."

"Oh crap!" Luke slapped his forehead. "Her surgery.

That was today?" He was such a dolt. "I'm sorry. I completely forgot. She didn't even say anything when I dropped off the twins this morning. How is she? How'd it go?"

"She's fine." The woman's voice was clipped. "Can I talk to you for a moment? In private?" She didn't wait for him to reply and he followed her back down the hallway into the front room.

It was probably about the kids. It was a common reaction among teachers, babysitters, doctors—everyone really—when they met his kids and then met him. With Luke's red hair and light blue eyes, it was a long-shot to assume he'd fathered any of his children. And while the oldest three *could* be related, Ophelia's dark complexion and Devon and Derrick's eyes identified them as being from different gene pools. She probably just wanted some clarification—to know the parameters of what the kids knew and what they didn't.

She stopped in the centre of the room and turned to him, hands on her hips, a deep furrow creasing her forehead.

Then again, she looked pissed. Not at him, surely? What could he have done to annoy her so completely? He'd only just arrived. She was probably worried about her mother. How could he have forgotten about Terry's surgery? "I'm very sorry."

"You said that already."

"Yes, I did. Terry told me you were coming to help with the kids during her convalescence. I really appreciate it. It's Monica, right?"

"Look, Mr. McMillan—"

"Luke," he said, flashing his most earnest smile.

"Luke," she repeated, frowning slightly, "we need to get a few things straight. This is a business with very clear hours of operation—not only for my sake but for the children's. You are aware that they are to be picked up by five-thirty and if not, there is a financial penalty of one dollar for every minute thereafter. You are forty-five minutes late. Forty-five times six is two hundred and seventy dollars that you owe. I won't charge you for the extra meals—this time."

"That's very generous of you," he said dryly. *Is she serious?* Like hell he was going to pay her two hundred and seventy dollars. Terry never worried if he was a few minutes late.

"As long as we understand each other."

Luke didn't understand her at all, but he sensed now wasn't the time to get into it. He needed this daycare. He'd tried working at home while his kids were around, and it had been a dismal failure for all of them. Two months, Terry had said; he could do this for two months. He'd just have to make sure he kept better track of his time—otherwise he'd go broke.

"Why don't you join us for dinner?" she said when he didn't comment further. "We have lots."

"Thank you." He could put the few bucks he'd save on this meal toward his debt to her.

At Monica's request, Michael rose and set a place at the table for Luke. It was a lively meal with the children relaying all of the day's events to their father. Monica had obviously heard the stories earlier because every once in a while she would remind them of an omitted detail.

She had a no-nonsense approach to the children's behaviour, while still exhibiting warmth and compassion.

When, after dinner, she asked for help with the dishes, she managed to find a job perfectly suited to each and every one of them—even Luke, who was given responsibility for sweeping the floor.

"Thank you for dinner, Monica," Luke said when the last dish was put away and the counters were wiped clean. "Now, I think I need to get these kids home so we can get to work on their homework."

"It's all done," Kate said. "We did it before dinner."

"Even your math?" Kate had been struggling in the subject lately and, although Luke was pretty good at math himself, he was at a loss to understand the new methods the teachers used.

"Oh yes." Kate beamed. "Monica is a whiz at math. She explained it so brilliantly it makes perfect sense to me now."

Monica stood behind Kate and put her hands on the girl's shoulders. "I just gave you a little direction. You figured it out on your own." She bent and kissed her temple, then looked up at Luke. "I'm a financial planner, so I deal with numbers all the time."

"I thought Terry said you were an early childhood educator?" Luke was taken aback by how easily this woman had slipped into his children's confidence.

"I was. I guess I still am. I *do* have the credentials, if that's what you're worried about."

"No, I'm not worried. Just..." He ran his hand through his hair, stumped about what to say next. Whatever it was, she'd likely take offence.

Well, she didn't have to like him, did she? He had worked very well with people who hadn't liked him, and with some he hadn't particularly liked, either. As long as

Monica Stevens was good to his kids that was all that mattered.

Except it wasn't.

As he drove his family home, he realized he wanted very much for her to like him, too. It was an unsettling feeling.

THREE

This was the last place Monica ever imagined setting foot in again. She glanced around the brightly lit lobby of the Kingston hospital. How many hours...days... weeks had she spent within these walls? She gave herself a mental shake to dispel the shroud of misery that was descending. It was water under the bridge now. She wasn't here for herself, but to visit her mother.

Cathy was across the lobby asking one of the silver-haired volunteers for Terry's room number. Her husband, Phil, had dropped them at the doorway and was trying to find a parking spot that wouldn't "break the bank." Monica remembered that problem, too.

"Monica?"

She froze. *Please, no.*

She turned slowly, praying she was mistaken, that, perhaps, being here had conjured up his memory. But no, there he stood in real life, looking as handsome and self-confident as she always remembered him.

"Jeff? Wow!" She hoped the smile she forced would

hide her shock. The blood had drained from her face and her body moved sluggishly toward him. What kind of hell had she fallen into?

His embrace was solid. Always the athlete, he hadn't let himself go as he'd aged. She rested her cheek briefly against his shoulder and inhaled his familiar minty scent. Then she pushed back and looked up at him, but couldn't think of a single thing to say.

"I heard you were coming back to help run the daycare while your mother was in the hospital," he said. "You look great. The west coast certainly agrees with you."

He'd always been quick with a compliment, yet she knew he was being sincere. Jeff, truly, was a nice guy. Growing up in the same village, she'd known him all her life, although they hadn't started dating until they'd both left home to go to university. He was studying business, and she was getting her childcare certification. They'd wanted the same things out of life: to have lots of kids and raise their family in Havenport. They'd married shortly after graduation. Jeff took over running his family's hardware store, and she worked in her mother's daycare while they tried to get pregnant.

They hadn't worried too much at first, but, as the months—and then years—went by without a baby, they knew something was wrong. And then it had begun: the doctor's visits, the procedures, the start of each month believing that this time it would be different. But it never was. The years of disappointment took their toll. She'd begged Jeff to consider adoption, but he wouldn't hear of it. He was an only child, and it was important to him— and his parents—that he have a biological offspring. Besides, *he* wasn't the problem.

The divorce papers hadn't come as a complete surprise. After all, they'd tried for fifteen years and she, at thirty-nine, was past her prime child-bearing years. It had been amicable. He'd been generous. But Monica couldn't stay. Everything in Havenport reminded her that she was broken, a woman unable to fulfill the most basic of womanly functions. Motherhood.

"The Island's great," she said. "No snow."

He chuckled. "Are you here to visit your mom? How is she?"

"Yeah. The surgery went well. We're just going up to see her now. What about you? What are you doing here?" She could have bitten her tongue.

"Well, ah…" Jeff played with the keys in his coat pocket and smiled nervously. "I'm here with Andrea." He nodded his head toward a very pregnant young woman seated in a wheelchair and watching them from across the lobby. "We're having a baby," he said unnecessarily. "Number four."

"Oh." Monica swallowed hard. "Congratulations."

"Yeah, thanks. Look I should get going. Her water's broke and we're heading up to the birthing unit. Maybe I can drop by and visit your mom later?"

"She'd like that."

Monica felt numb as Jeff wheeled his wife into an elevator and disappeared.

"You okay?" Cathy's touch on her shoulder broke her out of her daze.

"Sure," she said. "Why wouldn't I be?"

"What are the odds of him being here tonight?"

"Oh, I'd say they were pretty good," Monica said. She turned to her sister. "Four kids? Can you believe that? I would have thought one or two would have been enough to prove his virility—to demonstrate to everyone that *I* was the infertile one. Four is a little on the excessive side, wouldn't you say?"

Her sister didn't reply, but her raised eyebrow told Monica that, perhaps, she was over-reacting just a little bit.

"There's Phil." Cathy linked her arm and steered her toward the elevator.

"Hey, Mom," Monica bent down to kiss Terry's cheek. "How are you feeling?"

"Pretty good, all things considered." Terry winced as she tried to adjust her position. Both Cathy and Phil greeted her and then stood back so Monica could sit on the edge of the bed.

"Where are my granddaughters?" Terry said, looking toward the door. "I was hoping Jennifer and Stephanie would be with you."

"Sorry, they got a last-minute babysitting gig," Cathy said. "They're going to come by tomorrow."

"It's a little late for babysitting on a school night, don't you think?" Terry said.

Cathy laughed. "It's only eight-thirty, and besides, they're teenagers, they don't sleep at night anyway."

"I'm looking forward to spending some time with them while I'm here," Monica said. She'd been disappointed not to see her nieces in the vehicle when Cathy and Phil arrived to pick her up. She enjoyed spoiling the girls and flew them out to British Columbia to stay with her every spring break. "Maybe we'll take a road trip to Montreal for some shopping one of these weekends."

"They'd love that," Cathy said. "And better you than me."

"I wish I could go with you," Terry said wistfully.

Monica felt a twinge of guilt. There was nothing Terry liked more than shopping. It was a trait Monica and her two nieces seemed to have inherited, but for some reason, it had skipped Cathy entirely.

Her sister never seemed to want or need anything. Monica couldn't imagine what it would be like to feel so completely contented with what one already had in life.

"Well, we'll just have to go again before I leave," she said to her mother.

"How are you settling in, dear?" Terry asked. "Have you found everything you need?"

"Hah! Everything and more. You must have been shopping and cooking for the last month. I don't know if it's humanly possible to go through all the food you've got in the time I'm going to be here."

"You'd be surprised," Terry said. "Besides, the McMillan children often stay for dinner. Their father gets so busy he loses track of time."

"Yeah, I noticed that," Monica said dryly.

"So, what did you think of our Mr. McMillan?" Cathy asked.

"Oh yes, do tell," Terry said, grinning.

"Oh, please!" Phil groaned in the corner.

"You don't like him?" Monica was surprised. Phil was so easy-going it was difficult to imagine him not liking anyone.

"No, no, no. Luke's a great guy. What I don't like is the

way the women in this family go all googly-eyes over him."

"I don't go googly-eyes," Cathy said indignantly and turned to her mother. "Do I?"

"I think we all do, dear," Terry conceded. "Even Stephanie and Jennifer are a wee bit smitten with him."

"Well, you can count me out of the googly-eyes club," Monica said, giving Phil a thumb's up sign in solidarity. "I'm sure he's very nice, but our relationship is purely professional. I've made my expectations very clear, and it doesn't include extending the daycare's hours to accommodate his poor time management."

"Oh dear," Terry said, "you've already had a run-in. I hope you were pleasant."

"I am always pleasant, Mom. I'm just not going to allow myself to be taken advantage of."

"I doubt anyone would be foolish enough to try to take advantage of you, Ms Stevens, but rest assured, the message was received loud and clear."

Four heads swivelled toward the door and Monica cursed under her breath as Luke McMillan stood on the threshold, holding a large bouquet of fall flowers.

"Luke, how lovely," Terry said. "Are those for me?"

Monica glanced at her mother. *Yup, googly-eyes.* She stood up. "I'll go see if the nurses have a vase."

"No, you stay here," Cathy said. "Phil and I'll go. I want to talk to the nurses about when they're moving Mom to the convalescent home." Before Monica could stop her, Cathy had pulled her husband out of the room.

Looking for some way to be useful, Monica took the flowers from Luke and indicated for him to sit down beside her mother. She edged back toward the door, listening to them talk first about his kids and then the green community he was helping the town develop.

When Cathy returned, she was accompanied by a nurse who informed them it was time for the patient to go to sleep. Monica arranged the flowers while Cathy and Luke said goodbye to Terry, then she went to her mother's bedside.

"Good night, Mom." Monica kissed her mother's cheek. "I'll call you tomorrow to check on you."

Terry reached out and clasped her hand. "Thank you for coming back. I know it isn't easy."

"I'll be fine," Monica said, hoping she sounded more confident than she felt. How was she going to manage when everywhere she went she was reminded of her failure?

"I know you will." Terry squeezed her hand. "And be nice to Luke."

Monica rolled her eyes. "Good night."

Monica looked for Cathy in the hallway.

"Your sister and Phil took off. I said I'd drive you home," Luke said. "I was hoping we could talk."

"Oh? What about?"

"I don't know. The kids? Most people have a lot of questions when they meet them and then me."

She gazed up at him. Red hair, blue eyes, ruddy freckled skin. His wife might have been darker, but that wouldn't explain the origin of all his kids. She glanced at her watch. Nine-thirty—six-thirty back home. She was tired but doubted she'd be able to fall asleep for a few hours anyway. "Sure. Do you want to grab a coffee?"

There were few patrons in the hospital snack bar: a pair of nurses on a break and an older man completing a crossword puzzle. Monica watched through the glass partition as a very pregnant young woman, in a hospital gown, lumbered along the hallway. Her husband was trying to help her walk, but she impatiently shooed him away. She prayed they wouldn't come into the snack bar. They were too much of a reminder of Jeff and what was going on upstairs. She expelled a sigh of relief as they continued on past.

Luke set a Styrofoam cup of coffee in front of her. "Cream? Sugar?" He dumped a small pile of both onto the table.

"No, black's fine."

He nodded and sat down across from her. He picked up several of the sugar packages, ripped them open in a single motion, and poured them into his cup. He kept his head down, deep in thought, as he stirred his coffee. Finally, he looked up. "They all know they're adopted if you're wondering," he said. "They were toddlers when they came to us—all of them except the twins."

"Your wife...?" She didn't know how to phrase the question: Were any of them hers from a previous relationship?

"No." He shook his head. "Beth wasn't their biological mother, either."

"I see. That's all I need to know." She felt like a voyeur peering into his private life. Some things were personal and should be kept that way. Wasn't that the very reason she'd left Havenport to find a new life on the western shores of Canada?

"Actually, if you're going to be spending so much time with them, I'd like you to know the whole story, where they each came from and why."

The coffee tasted foul, but Monica forced herself to swallow it. "Okay, if that's what you want, but it won't make any difference to how I treat them."

Luke opened another two sugar pouches and poured them into his coffee.

"I don't think that's going to help," she said. "The coffee's pretty awful."

He smiled and continued stirring the sugar in his coffee. "I met Beth when we were working for an aid agency in Africa. We fell in love and got married. For the next ten years, we travelled the world doing international development work and trying to start a family." He took a sip of coffee and grimaced.

"For ten years?" Sympathy stirred in her chest. She knew that routine.

"Not all ten, no. About five, I guess. At first, we figured it was the lifestyle, and we were okay with that. But then we got serious about having kids—we were getting older, you know. We got checked out and discovered Beth had an abnormally formed uterus; it was genetic, she was born with it, and it meant she couldn't become pregnant."

A cause. A real cause. What Monica wouldn't have given to have been provided with a reason for her inability to conceive a child? Instead, all she'd gotten was medical mumbo-jumbo about idiopathic infertility and how she was among the twenty per cent of barren women for whom a reason cannot be found. And without a definitive reason, month after month she allowed herself to hope.

"It must have been difficult for you," she said, remembering the divorce papers and the point at which she'd given up.

"It was. We threw ourselves back into our work and that was fine for a few years."

"What made you decide it wasn't enough; that you wanted to adopt?"

He took another sip of coffee, shook his head in disgust and pushed the cup away. "I had accepted that we'd never have a family, and I thought Beth had, too. But we were working in the Baltic, helping to rebuild a school, when we encountered a young boy, an orphan, who was being cared for by several grandmothers in the community. His whole family was dead."

"Michael?"

Luke nodded. "I saw the way she looked at him, watching his every move. If he fell, she'd rush to his side. She was always looking for him, trying to find some way to interact with him. That's when I realized she wasn't okay with not having children. So, I talked to the grandmothers and the community leaders, and we applied to the proper government officials to adopt Michael. It took a while, but when we left the Baltic, we were a family of three."

"He's adapted to Canada very well," she said. "You'd never know he wasn't born here."

"Yeah." Luke's face lit up with love. "He's a great kid."

"What about the others?"

"Well, with a young son we couldn't very well go traipsing all over the world anymore. We came back to Ontario, to Havenport, and settled down. We realized there must be more kids that needed a good, stable home with loving parents. We contacted some local adoption agencies, and it was through one of them we got Kate, Lucy, and Ophelia. Not all at the same time, of course, but over the next few years." His expression turned wistful. "We were so blessed. I thought we had the perfect family."

"And then you decided to adopt two more?"

"Not exactly." He chuckled and then became more serious. "I was asked to consult on a project in Eurasia. While I was there, I met two orphan babies who needed a home, and I just knew they belonged with us. They completed our family."

"Did you never feel the need to have your own children?"

"Do you mean biologically?" He appeared taken aback by the question. "I wanted children with my wife. She was unable to conceive, so this was the only way to do that. The fact that we aren't genetically related is irrelevant. I couldn't love my kids any more, regardless of how they came into this world." He frowned. "You seem surprised."

"I guess I am. That's not been my experience with men. The ones I've known seem to have some sort of primeval imperative to provide DNA to their children.'

"Then I'd suggest you've been hanging out with the wrong men."

Monica's tried to smile but couldn't quite manage it. A few floors above them her ex-husband was fulfilling his dream of becoming a father—again. It had taken him two wives to do it. Wrong man, indeed. "You're probably right."

Luke stood. "I should get you home. You're going to have two high-spirited little boys to take care of tomorrow."

"I'm looking forward to it," she said, and was surprised to realize she really was. When she arrived, she'd been dreading facing young children day in and day out, a constant reminder of what she couldn't have. But talking to Luke made her wonder if Jeff's selfishness didn't deserve a larger share of the responsibility for their childlessness. There were all kinds of families if one was open-minded enough. "And you know that two hundred and seventy dollars? Let's just forget about it."

FOUR

"Not too high," Monica called to Devon and Derrick. The boys had left the slushy mud puddle they'd been excavating with toy backhoes to scamper over to the tire swing. Monica rolled the pair of trucks out of the middle of the muck and up onto the last clean patch of snow. They were certainly keeping her busy, but it had been years since she'd had this much fun.

She glanced down at her mud-soaked jeans and shook her head. If only her clients could see her now! They'd never recognize their perfectly coifed, always serious, financial adviser in the dishevelled mess she'd become.

Over the last few weeks, life had settled into a predictable pattern. Luke took his older children to their school bus and then brought Devon and Derrick to the daycare. Sometimes he stayed for a cup of coffee but usually, he was rushing to a meeting. He claimed he was trying to get his work done within normal hours to adhere to Monica's strict schedule, but he rarely made it back before six o'clock. She didn't complain—he was doing his best—and she enjoyed the children's company. If she was honest, she enjoyed Luke's company, too, but that wasn't why she often insisted he and the children stay for dinner.

Kristoff, the gander, ventured out from behind the bird barn, where he kept watch over the rest of the flock at the pond, to check on his other charges—the twins. He and Monica had come to an uneasy truce, perhaps each recognizing they shared a common concern for the boys. She still wasn't happy to be saddled with a gaggle of geese, but she'd assigned each child a bird—Devon and Derrick shared Kristoff—so her involvement with them was minimal. The kids had risen to the challenge and seemed to relish their new responsibilities, not even complaining when they had to clean out the bird barn.

"Devon! I said—"

She wasn't sure if the unholy scream came from her or Kristoff as Derrick flew out of the tire swing and tumbled head-first onto the ground. The mud sucked at her feet, tripping her twice as she raced to him. He lay motionless while Devon stood beside him, pale and on the verge of tears.

"It's okay, Devon," She tried to soothe the boy, but her real focus was on Derrick. She knelt beside him. "Derrick?" She only had time to check that he was breathing before she heard him moan. *Thank goodness.* "Derrick, can you hear me?"

His eyes fluttered open and he winced. "My head hurts."

"I'm not surprised," she said. "That was quite a fall you took."

"Yeah, it was wicked wild," Devon said, his tears gone. "You were flying."

She scowled at Devon. "Little boys are not supposed to fly. He could have been seriously hurt." She turned back to Derrick. "Can you sit up?"

"I think so." He slowly raised himself up. "Was I really flying, Devie?"

"There will be no more flying!" That tire swing was coming down right away, Monica decided. She'd never been one of those childcare workers who advocated banning swing sets and monkey bars in a misguided attempt to protect kids from themselves, but this hit too close to home. She'd been right there watching and, still, Derrick could have…She didn't want to think about it.

"My head is thumping," Derrick said.

She peered closer and gingerly prodded his scalp. There was a bump forming on the right side of his head. She suspected that under his dark hair there would be one heck of a bruise. But could he have a concussion? "Let's go inside," she said. "I'll make you some hot chocolate while I call the doctor."

"Am I sick?" Derrick asked, unsteadily rising to his feet.

"I don't think so, but I do think Dr. Myer should have a look at that bump, just to make sure."

"I'm sorry, Derry," Devon said, following them into the house. "I pushed too hard, and you got hurt."

"It's okay. I got to fly."

Her first call, to Luke, went straight to voice mail. She simply asked him to call her cell phone as soon as possible. The next call wasn't any more effective. The McMillan's pediatrician was away at a conference and her office "strongly suggested" she take Derrick to the hospital to get him checked out immediately.

Monica glanced at her watch. What were the odds they'd get to the hospital, see a doctor, and be back before the rest of the kids got home? She regretted calling Cathy at work, but it couldn't be helped. Surely the school would understand that this was an emergency.

She strapped the boys into their car seats and cranked the engine on the daycare's large white van. She hated driving the thing, partly because of its size—it could hold fifteen—and partly because of the enormous cartoon goose painted on both side panels. But it was already equipped with child car seats and her rental wasn't.

The boys' animated conversation behind her should have reassured Monica that Derrick was going to be fine, but she continued to feel guilty. This had happened while she was looking after him. She pressed a little harder on the gas pedal.

It wasn't until she ushered the boys into the emergency room and saw the startled looks from staff and patients that she considered how the three of them must appear. They hadn't taken the time to do more than wash their hands after their outdoor adventure; all were still dressed in their mud-stained clothes.

Although she didn't have his health card with her—something she needed to rectify the next time she saw Luke—the mere possibility of a concussion moved Derrick to the front of the emergency patient line. He was quickly seen by a resident and taken to be x-rayed. And then they waited. And waited.

Monica had grabbed the bag of colouring books and games that her mother always kept in the van, but after three hours she was finding it difficult to keep the boys entertained. What was taking so long?

She'd called Luke several more times, leaving messages updating him on their latest status, but he still hadn't returned her calls.

Finally, the resident they'd originally seen called them into one of the private cubicles to meet with the senior doctor. Derrick was fine, he said. There wasn't cause to suspect a concussion, but she needed to keep an eye on him for the next few days. If the headache persisted, or if he had vision problems, she was to bring him right back.

Relieved and exhausted, she didn't have the energy to argue with the boys when they pleaded for her to take them to the local fast-food restaurant for hamburgers. None of them had eaten for hours, and she agreed they had been "extremely good and deserved a treat."

She was strapping them into their car seats when Luke bellowed from across the hospital parking lot. "Monica!"

He streaked toward them like a man on fire, not even trying to dodge the puddles. Monica glanced down at his feet. Tomorrow he'd be tossing out those fancy shoes.

"I wish you'd have called," she said as he approached. "You could have saved yourself a trip. Derrick is just fine."

"You had no right!" His eyes were wild, and his hair was a tangled mess. His red face stood in sharp contrast to the crisp whiteness of his dress shirt. Who knows where his jacket and coat were? His tie was askew, too.

She stepped aside as he approached the van. Through the window, she watched the twin's initial pleasure at seeing their father become muted when they saw his expression. Then Derrick spoke. "I went flying, Daddy."

Monica groaned. "It wasn't quite like that."

Luke whirled toward her. "What were you thinking bringing them here? How dare you?"

What the...? "Over there." She pointed away from the vehicle. "Be right back, boys."

As she led Luke away from the van she could hear the boys calling out: "Don't be mad, Daddy." "Is Monica in trouble?"

She turned to him. "Now, can you please explain, in a civilized tone, exactly what your problem seems to be?"

"Those are my children. I am the one who decides what treatment they are to receive."

His face turned even redder if that was possible. He was heaving deep, heavy breaths, and swaying slightly. If she wasn't so taken aback by his comment she might have suggested she take *him* to the emergency. He looked like he was having some sort of attack.

"If you had bothered to answer your phone any one of the dozen times I called you, you could have had a say in Derrick's treatment." She spoke slowly, her tone measured.

"They have a doctor. They didn't have to come here."

"And if you had bothered to listen to the messages I left you, you would know that Dr. Myer is out of town and her office said to come here."

"You should have tried harder to get hold of me."

"Excuse me if I was a little busy taking care of *your* children."

"Well, it's after five-thirty. You're off the clock."

Monica watched dumbfounded as Luke strode over to the van, unstrapped Devon and Derrick, and carried them away. She smiled and waved to reassure the boys that everything was all right, but inside she was seething and confused.

What had just happened? She'd never seen Luke so angry before. She'd never seen him angry at all; never even heard him raise his voice.

What had she done wrong? Aside from allowing one of his children to become injured and require medical attention, of course.

She climbed into the van. Her hands shook as she tried to insert the key into the ignition. She'd been so afraid when she saw Derrick immobile on the ground. She'd been scared he was seriously injured, or worse, and upset with herself for allowing it to happen. It would have been easy to lash out at Devon for pushing his brother too high, and perhaps if he hadn't been a small child, she might have exorcized her fear and anger on him.

Imagine what Luke had felt when he heard that his son had been injured and taken to hospital? He must have been terrified.

Monica took a deep breath and exhaled slowly. Surely, that was all there was to it.

LUKE LOOKED DOWN at the number on his call display: *L. Burkholder.*

Crap! After today's fiasco, there was no way he couldn't take this call, regardless of the time. He took a deep breath and pressed the answer button. "Ms. Burkholder."

"Mr. McMillan, I'm surprised you're answering your phone. Usually, I get shunted off to voice mail."

"I apologize. I've just been very busy. You know how it is with balancing work and family. There are never enough hours in the day to do everything that has to be done." He tried to infuse his voice with the honey-sweetness Beth had always accused him of using to unfairly get his way.

"It's your busy-ness that concerns me." Her voice was clipped, no fly to his honey. "It would be a challenge even for a married couple to raise so many children."

He tried the no-nonsense, professional approach. "I can assure you that my children are not suffering from my work schedule. I've arranged excellent care—"

"We've been through this all before, Mr. McMillan. Mother Goose Daycare has an excellent reputation; that's not the problem. It's *your* ability to handle the responsibility at issue."

He closed his eyes. He could imagine Lydia Burkholder sitting in her tiny cubicle somewhere in the Ontario social services office, surrounded by pictures of her cats and solo trips to exotic locations. He'd never met the woman—hoped he'd never have to—but he doubted very much that she had children of her own. If she did, she'd understand why keeping his family together was so important to him.

"Take for example your son's visit to the hospital this afternoon."

Darn it! He knew that was going to come back to bite him. If only Monica hadn't taken Derrick to the public hospital. He knew the twins' file was flagged and social services would be notified.

"Derrick had a fall. He was taken there as a precaution. He is perfectly fine."

"Yes, thank goodness. But that's not what I'm getting at. Why couldn't the hospital get hold of you? They tried for hours but eventually gave up. I told them to return the boys to Ms. Stevens' care so they could go home."

"It was an unusual and isolated incident."

"I'd like to think that was the case, Mr. McMillan, but my inability to speak with you for the last month makes me think otherwise."

"I can assure you, it won't happen again." He was pleading for his family. How could he make her understand?

"No, it won't. And I'm not going to go away. You can either help me or not, it's up to you, but I am going to do my job. I will be in touch to arrange a face-to-face meeting."

Luke stared out the front window of his home trying to figure a way out of this mess. The streetlight illuminated the softly falling snow. It was coming down in big puffy flakes, gently swirling, before landing on the ground. It was beautiful. Peaceful. But it wasn't going to last. There was a storm coming off the lake. It wouldn't be long before the tranquil scene turned into a vicious tempest.

He knew Lydia Burkholder had a job to do, but did she have to be so dogmatic about it? Couldn't she see she was threatening to break up a family? He loved his kids, and he thought he was a pretty good father. They were far better off with him than they would have been if he and Beth hadn't taken them in—especially Derrick and Devon. He knew that for certain.

Darn it, Monica.

Maybe he should have been completely up front with

her when he'd told her about where the twins came from. At least, then, she would have understood why they couldn't go to the hospital.

Or would she? She'd softened over the weeks he'd come to know her, but she still retained that by-the-book mindset she'd shown when he'd first met her.

It was too late for second-guessing now. Luke and his kids would have to live with the consequences of today. But there was no way he was going to give up fighting to keep his family together.

FIVE

Monica took a sip of her coffee and grimaced. It had gone cold while she'd been staring out the kitchen window, watching the freshly fallen snow being whipped into a frenzy by the wind coming off the lake.

It had started snowing just as she returned home from the hospital and had kept it up most of the following day. Luke had called the next morning to say he was working at home and would keep the boys with him. While she fully understood the desire of a parent to keep his children close after narrowly escaping harm, a part of her worried he was still angry with her for taking Derrick to the hospital. She tried to convince herself she was being overly sensitive to his reaction, but he'd been brusque and distant on the phone.

Monica poured the stale coffee into the sink. She'd spent her unexpected free day curled up on the sofa reading, venturing outside only to feed Kristoff and his friends. Today, however, she needed to dig her little car out of the snowbank and clear the laneway. It was Saturday, so she couldn't count on help from the McMillan kids. She was on her own.

She shivered as a mighty gust rattled the window pane. With the end of the snow came a sudden drop in temperature. The radio said it wasn't going to climb above freezing for the next few days and Monica was unprepared. After seven years on temperate Vancouver Island, she'd forgotten how quickly winter could arrive in Havenport. It was the middle of November.

If she'd been smart, she would have bought some winter clothes when she'd taken Jennifer and Stephanie shopping in Montreal, last weekend. But that trip had been about spoiling the girls, not practical clothes shopping for herself.

She mentally ran through her current wardrobe. Although she'd brought her warmest clothes with her, there was nothing that was up to the current weather conditions. Her mother's winter coat and boots were at the convalescent centre where outdoor walking was part of Terry's rehabilitation.

Monica stood on tip-toes, rummaging around the top shelf of the closet. Surely there had to be something. Her hands brushed against a soft fabric, and she pulled it forward, grinning as she recognized the pink faux-fur and leather mitten. She jumped to try to claim its mate, succeeding after several attempts. Along with the second mitten came a boldly striped orange, yellow, and fuchsia wool scarf.

She knew her mother was a pack rat, but this was crazy. Monica had worn these mittens and scarf in college more than twenty years ago. They couldn't have been on that shelf since then. Terry must have retrieved them from storage more recently. Maybe there was more up in the attic?

Monica climbed the stairs to the third floor and scanned the neatly arranged attic. *Mom might be a pack rat, but thank heavens she was a well-organized one.* Labelled boxes were stacked along three of the walls, while old furniture was lined up along the fourth.

She walked over to what was obviously her section— her name prominent in bold black marker—removed the lid from one of the boxes and squealed when she saw what it contained. She opened the box beside it and shook her head in disbelief. Had her mother kept her *entire* high school wardrobe?

She picked up the slinky lavender slip dress—it was a wonder Terry let her out of the house wearing that—and tossed it aside when she saw her favourite over-sized acid wash jeans. And her black lace, fingerless gloves! Oh, how she'd loved those things.

As she plowed through the boxes, each garment brought back memories. The stretch-stirrup pants, the oversized tops, the gel shoes, the neon-coloured leg warmers...

"Hello? Monica? Are you up here?"

She leapt to her feet and turned toward the attic's staircase.

Luke's eyes widened as he took in Monica's full 1990s attire. "I did ring the b-b-bell." His snicker turned into a full belly laugh. "Kn-nocked. And I c-c-c-alled for—" He took a deep breath and finally seemed to get himself under control. "Sorry, I didn't mean to interrupt your trip down memory lane. Did you really used to dress like that?"

She glanced down at her outfit. Her body wasn't quite the same as it had been in high school, but everything still fit for the most part. The black stirrup pants were a little tighter around the belly and looser in the hips, but the overly large red sweater covered that nicely. "I think the striped leg warmers are a nice touch, don't you?" She struck a pose and grinned. "I miss leg warmers."

"Who needs solar power when you've got those. There's enough wattage there to supply the whole county," he said moving to stand in the centre of the room. He cocked his head to the side as his gaze slowly scanned the length of her. "You must have had all the boys chasing you in high school."

"Oh, hardly," she scoffed, embarrassed by his scrutiny. "I didn't date in high school. I didn't even have a proper date for prom. It was just a big group of us."

"I find that difficult to believe."

Monica shrugged. "Don't get me wrong. I had a great time in high school—lots of friends. Just no *boy*friends."

"I guess I just assumed you and Jeff dated in high school, since you're both from here and lived here after you married."

She shouldn't have been surprised Luke knew about her and Jeff. Havenport was a small town and gossip was its lifeblood. How many times had she returned from school with information for Terry only to learn that her mother already heard it through the local grapevine?

"No. He never gave me a second glance in high school. As the star centre of the region's hockey team, he was way out of my league. We didn't start dating until we met, again, in university. By then he'd given up his dream of being drafted by the NHL and wanted to move home, start a family, and take over his parent's store." She stopped. That made her sound bitter, and she wasn't. She was just being realistic about the situation. "That didn't come out right."

"I didn't have much luck dating in high school, either."

"Oh, come on," she said. "You're just trying to make me feel better."

"No, it's true. Red hair, pimply face, scrawny body. It was not a pretty picture."

Monica tried to reconcile the tall, broad-shouldered, athletic man in front of her with his description of his younger self. "I guess we were just a couple of ugly ducklings."

"It's too bad we didn't know each other in high school. We could have kept each other company while we waited to turn into the swans we've become." He reached into his pocket and took out his cell phone.

"Checking on the kids?"

"No," he said, not raising his head. He fumbled with the phone for a few moments more, then looked up and grinned.

She faintly heard the banging drum beat and horns of the Spice Girls' "Stop." Luke turned up the volume and then placed the phone down on a box.

"Gotta love the Internet. There's a music stream for every situation." He took a step toward her and held out his hand. "Wanna dance?"

Monica allowed the music to move through her as she and Luke danced through Spice Girls, REM's "Losing my Religion," and NSYNC's "Bye, Bye, Bye." She hadn't heard this music in years. It brought back feelings of being young and free, and a sense of the wild abandon she'd experienced on the high school dance floor.

The mood shifted as the attic filled with the first strains of "Waterfall" by TLC. That, too, brought back high school memories of those awkward moments when you didn't know if the boy you were dancing with was willing to slow dance with you or if he was going to high-tail it back to his friends, abandoning you on the dance floor.

Luke didn't hesitate. He wrapped both arms around her waist as if it was the most natural thing in the world. She reached up to encircle his neck and rested her head against his chest. She could hear his heart beating, steady and firm. He was steady and firm. He smelled wonderful, a mixture of his woodsy aftershave with the softly sweet vanilla scent of the soap used by both him and his children.

He was a good dancer, his moves confident and clear. It was obviously something he'd done a lot of. Jeff hadn't liked to dance—typical jock—and she'd missed it during their time together—and after. How long since she'd been held on a dance floor? Held anywhere, for that matter?

A good dancer. A good husband. A good father. Why couldn't she have met Luke, or someone like him, twenty years ago?

"Waterfall" morphed into another slow song. He stopped moving but didn't release her. She looked up and gazed into his clear blue eyes. Her breath caught in her throat as she saw his pupils expand with a growing desire. His head had barely started to lower when she raised hers to meet him.

She'd anticipated the kiss, but not the scorching volt of

electricity that swept through her when their lips touched. This was unlike any first kiss she'd experienced.

It wasn't tentative. It wasn't gentle. Luke's lips seared hers with an intense, demanding heat, and she hungrily responded. When his tongue claimed entry, she eagerly took it, tasting his flavours of peppermint and coffee.

Wanting more, she wound his red curls around her fingers and pulled his head closer.

His hands had lowered to her hips, massaging them and grinding against her to the beat of Phil Collin's "Just Another Day in Paradise." He was slowly pushing her backwards until she felt the wall of boxes against her legs. She arched toward him and he lifted her onto the waist-high pile.

It happened so quickly. Her lips were torn away from Luke's, and she felt herself falling. Her arms windmilled as she tried to grab onto something… anything. She jolted to a hard stop, her bottom securely lodged in a box with her legs sticking up in the air.

"Jeez, Monica. Are you all right?" He grabbed her arm and hauled her to her feet. "I'm sorry."

She looked down at the collapsed boxes and then back up at Luke. His face was red as if from exertion, and he was breathing heavily.

She was breathing pretty heavily herself. *What just happened?* And she wasn't thinking about her fall into the box. "I'm fine," she lied.

She didn't know what to do next. A moment ago, they'd been sharing a passionate kiss that had the potential to…to what? She looked away. Would she really have had sex in her mother's attic with a man she'd known for only a few weeks?

"I hope we didn't break anything valuable," he said.

"Nah." Breaking what was in the box was the least of her worries. If Luke could have such a devastating effect on her physically, what could he do to her emotionally? Already she felt herself grow weak-kneed every time she saw him with his kids or thought about how he had loved his wife so much he'd agreed to adopt their family.

She looked back at him. He looked so serious, so worried. "Besides," she said, pointing to the bold black letters written on the boxes in the tumble-down pile, "this is Cathy's stuff."

THAT WAS UNEXPECTED.

Luke turned the snow blower around and headed back up the driveway. He'd come to the Stevens' house to apologize for getting upset with Monica in the hospital parking lot. Once he'd calmed down, he'd come to the realization she hadn't made things worse. Not really. He couldn't have avoided Lydia Burkholder much longer, anyway.

He'd also brought over some winter clothes and boots that had belonged to Beth. He didn't know what Monica had in the way of winter wear, but he suspected her west coast wardrobe wasn't up to Eastern Ontario's current weather conditions. They were meant to be a peace offering.

He'd offered to clear the lane as an excuse to get out into the cool air and think. Unfortunately, Monica had insisted on helping. So, with each return trip up the drive-way, he watched her clearing the paths between the house, the garage and the bird barn, and remembered the taste of her luscious lips and the impression of her sweet body pressed against his.

He breathed a sigh of relief, the band around his chest releasing as she disappeared around the corner of the bird barn.

He hadn't meant to kiss her. He had no business kissing her. But there was something about their dancing that had made him forget, for a short while, that he was a father to six children, that he was in danger of losing his family. Hell, she'd even made him forget about Beth. He couldn't remember a time since her death when he'd done anything and not thought about the last time he had done it with his wife.

He couldn't get romantically involved with Monica. She had made it very clear she was anxious to return to her financial career, back in British Columbia, just as soon as Terry was well enough to come home and run the daycare.

A short-term fling was out of the question, too. As much as he'd love to make love to her, explore every inch of the lush body he'd barely tasted, he'd sworn he'd never parade a series of women through his children's lives.

Monica reappeared, and he sharply turned the snow blower around, not that she could see his erection from this distance, but it made him feel like a school boy caught fantasizing about the girl next door.

In any event, he had no idea how Monica felt about the kiss. Oh, she'd enjoyed it, that much was certain. But as to whether she'd be game for anything more? He shook his head at his foolishness. No point even going there.

Unless she decided to stay.

SIX

Monica carefully placed the pile of dessert plates into the sink's soapy water. The house was quiet, seeming even more so after the commotion of the day.

Beside her, Luke lifted a glass from the drying rack and ran a towel around the inside before wandering off to return it to its place in the cupboard. Her body thrummed with awareness as he moved easily around the kitchen. Could he hear her heart pounding into the silence?

Everyone else had left but he'd insisted on staying to help her clean up Lucy's birthday dinner dishes. It was the first time they'd been alone since their kiss more than a week ago. She hadn't known how she'd react. What would she say? How would she feel? While Luke had given no indication their kiss had changed anything for him, she was in a constant state of anticipation whenever he was around. And when he wasn't, he—and his kiss—were constantly on her mind.

Today he seemed different, though. Quieter, more pensive. It was probably the birthday celebration—they were always the toughest after a loss. Birthdays. Thanks-giving. Christmas. Each punctuated the absence, a specific point in time where you could remember everything you did with the other person. Or, in Monica's case, every-thing you didn't do.

The day had been everything she'd ever imagined a child's birthday celebration to be. She knew she should be elated that she'd experienced hosting one at least once in her life—and she was. It was just that her happiness was cut by the bittersweet awareness that it would never happen again. Oh, she could return for a visit, but it wouldn't be the same. The closeness she had with the McMillan children—with Luke—wouldn't be there. You can't maintain that from five thousand kilo-metres away.

"Monica?" He was staring at her, worry creasing his forehead. "Are you okay?"

She glanced away from him, afraid her eyes would betray what she'd been thinking. The drying rack was empty. "Sorry, just daydreaming, I guess. It was a great day." She picked up a soapy plate, rinsed it, and put it in the rack.

"It was perfect. I can't thank you enough for all you did to make this day so special for Lucy—for all of us."

She nodded and rinsed another plate. It had been perfect. Her mother, Cathy, and her two nieces had arrived early in the morning to begin the preparations. Terry had been propped up on a recliner and made comfortable so she could supervise the kitchen. She was thrilled to be out of the convalescent home—even for a day—and even more pleased to be passing on her family recipes to her granddaughters. Phil arrived around noon and positioned himself in front of the television for an afternoon of hockey.

It had been Monica's idea to include her mother and Cathy's family in the birthday celebrations. The McMillan children, she said, desperately wanted to see their Nanny Goose. All week long, Derrick and Devon had been making a welcome home banner in her honour.

The arrival of Luke and his six children was made even more boisterous by the "get better gift" they brought with them. As they unloaded the crate, Monica stared in horror at the large white and brown goose loudly protesting her captivity.

"The boys saw it in the market this morning and thought it might be nice for Kristoff to have a partner again," Luke said apologetically.

"Her name is Anna," Ophelia said, clapping her hands.

"That makes sense," Monica said, smiling weakly. Cathy had been correct. Monica was sure she could now sing all the songs and recite the entire dialogue for both *Frozen* and *Frozen II* without prompts.

Kristoff appeared from behind the bird barn, no doubt attracted by the noisy arrival. Derrick and Devon were vibrating in anticipation. "Let 'er out, let 'er out," they chorused.

Luke bent down and released the latch. Anna stepped out of the crate and everyone held their breath as Kristoff ambled toward her. He paused when he got close, cocked his head, issued a loud squawk, then turned and waddled back toward the barn with Anna following closely behind.

"I think she was supposed to be somebody's dinner," Monica grumbled to Cathy as they headed into the house. "She's not even the same type of goose as the others."

"Don't be a spoilt-sport. Besides, you know what her arrival means?"

"No, what?"

"Oh, come on," Cathy chided. "Christmas is only a month away. Now we have *six* geese."

"Just as long as they don't start a-laying," Monica said and then laughed. Her sister's glass-half-full attitude was contagious. What difference did one more goose make if it made the kids happy?

"Let's take a break." Luke's voice interrupted her thoughts.

She glanced down and realized she'd stopped washing the dishes again. "Okay. I'll finish up in the morning. There isn't much left."

She followed him down the hall toward the entrance. She expected him to collect his coat and leave but instead, he turned into the front room, sat down, and motioned for her to join him on the sofa.

"Your mother's doing well. I expect she'll be home soon."

His words drove a knife into Monica's heart. When she'd arrived, she'd been hoping for Terry's speedy recovery so she could get back to her safe, quiet life on Vancouver Island. Now, the thought of leaving brought physical anguish. "Yes, she's a tough one. The doctors expect she'll be home before Christmas."

"And what about you?" He shifted to face her.

"Me? What do you mean?"

"When your mother returns, will you leave right away? Or will you stay for the holidays?"

She lowered her head, allowing her hair to fall forward so he wouldn't see her despair. "I don't know."

"The kids would like it if you stayed." He brushed back her hair, tucking it behind her ears, and cupping her face. "*I* would like it if you stayed."

She raised her gaze to his and felt the tickle of a traitorous teardrop fall across her cheek. "For Christmas?" she whispered hoarsely.

"Or longer."

He lowered his head and softly kissed away the tear. She tasted her own salty agony on his lips as he moved to claim her mouth. Unlike last time, this kiss was gentle, his lips like butterfly wings against hers. He quietly played with her mouth; his teeth nipped, his tongue explored, but he didn't demand entry. He just teased until she couldn't take it anymore. All evening her body had been on edge, attentive to his every move. She hadn't known what she wanted from him—at least nothing she'd admit to herself —until now.

She raised her hands to his head and threaded her fingers through his hair, encouraging him to deepen the kiss. She moaned, deep and low, as she opened her mouth to receive his tongue and savoured the taste of him.

She arched toward him, loving the hardness of his chest and the power of his arms as they wrapped around her, pulling her closer. Then he grabbed her hips and shifted her beneath him on the sofa. The length of his long, lean body lying on top of hers was pure heaven.

He gazed down at her, passion turning his eyes deep midnight. "I haven't been able to stop thinking about you," he whispered, tracing his finger across her cheek and over her lips.

Her breath caught, and before she could reply he reclaimed her mouth. With one arm propping him up to keep from crushing her, his other hand began a tortuously slow descent from her chin to her neck, along her collarbone, and down to the opening of her blouse, his lips following right behind. She could feel his single hand fumble with the buttons and smiled as she heard him utter a frustrated curse.

"Just rip it," she said, desperate to feel his hands on her body.

The tug of the fabric and the sound of buttons popping off and scattering along the floor sent a flood of damp heat between her thighs. She pulled at his shirt, bringing it over his head and tossing it aside. Her hands massaged the hard planes of his broad shoulders as she looked down at the erotic image of his red hair between her breasts. She could feel his hot breath on her chest as his fingers skimmed the edge of her bra.

His breath hitched as he whispered, "You are so beautiful." He crawled back up her body and took her in his arms. "I've dreamed of making love to you every night," he said, kissing her gently.

She rested her cheek against the soft red down on Luke's chest. She was in big trouble. How had this man gotten under her skin in a few short weeks? He was everything she had ever thought she wanted. And soon, she would have to leave him to return to her life in British Columbia. She heard a small whimper and realized it had come from her.

"What's wrong?" he asked. "Is this all too fast?"

"No," she said. "I was just thinking about your question of when I'm going to leave."

"Don't."

"Don't what? Think about it?"

"No." He sat up, pulling her with him. He stared intently into her eyes. "Don't leave."

"But my home is there."

"What do you have there? A job? A house? Some friends?" He took her hands. "Your family is here. Your mother would love for you to return to the daycare centre, and the kids love you. Stay here with us, Monica. Please."

She pulled her ripped blouse up over her shoulders. She wasn't self-conscious about her nakedness, but she needed a few minutes to try to process what he was asking of her.

"I'm making a mess of this. Let me try again." Luke slid off the sofa and knelt in front of her. He clasped her hands and earnestly looked up at her. "Monica Stevens, will you do me the great honour of becoming my wife?"

The room tilted as she gaped at him. They barely knew each other. But then again, hadn't she, only a few minutes ago, been thinking of him as the perfect mate?

"I can see I've taken you by surprise," he said ruefully. "I'm crazy about you. I think about you all the time. You're smart. You're funny. You're great with the kids—they love you." He looked down at his bulge in his pants and smiled sheepishly. "And if you couldn't already tell, I think you're sexy as hell."

"It's just so…so…sudden."

"That's the responsible early childhood educator talking." He stood and pulled her to her feet. He reached out to stroke her cheek and then bent to give her a searing kiss that had her head swimming and her toes curling. What that man could do with his tongue should be illegal.

"Let me take you upstairs and see if I can bring you around to my way of thinking on the subject."

Monica's heart fluttered at his mischievous smile. She'd heard he was a fierce negotiator, but she was far from being done with him. Her imagination envisioned all sorts of pleasurable scenarios in her bed. Still, the responsible early childhood educator's voice wouldn't be silenced. "Don't you have to get home to the kids?"

"Nope. Your sister's taken them for the night."

"The whole night?"

"The *whole* night."

He held out his hand and she took it willingly. "I might not be as easy to persuade as you think," she said.

"Then I'll have to make sure I try really, *really* hard."

SEVEN

"See, Monica? Kristoff and Anna are going to be married just like you and Daddy." Devon pointed to the two geese that were leading the gaggle from the bird barn down to a sunny spot by the pond.

The weather had been mild for the last week with the above-freezing temperatures and sunny days melting much, but not all, of the snow that had so far fallen this season. The reprieve from winter wasn't going to last, though. Forecasters were calling for a major drop in temperature with stormy weather predicted over the next few days.

The twins had become fixated on the idea of marriage ever since she and Luke told their families of their plan. She glanced down at the simple diamond on her finger and shook her head. It still felt like a dream.

They'd set Christmas Eve as the wedding date. She'd been afraid they were moving too quickly, but Luke had insisted he didn't want to wait. He said he was uncomfortable having a woman who was not his wife share his bed with his kids around—even if they were engaged—and it didn't feel right to leave the children with a sitter while he spent the night at Monica's home. After two weeks of nothing more than stolen kisses, she had to agree: the sooner the better.

Monica followed the twins down to the pond where they were preparing to officiate at another mock wedding for Kristoff and Anna. She hated to admit it, but the arrival of the new goose had been good for the gander. He seemed calmer now, less irritable, happier even—if it was possible to ascribe those characteristics to a bird.

In many ways, she felt the same way. While she'd initially worried that her attraction to Luke might have had more to do with his relationship with his children than as a man—he was a wonderful father—her doubts were erased after their night together. Luke was a passionate and considerate lover, making sure her desires were satisfied, as well as his own. When the sun had risen in the morning, she'd known beyond a shadow of a doubt she was in love and wanted to share the rest of her life with him.

She wasn't naive. She knew his children were part of the reason she'd fallen for him, but being a father was a large measure of the man he was. She felt privileged that he cared so much for her that he wanted to include her in his family.

Of course, her friends on the west coast thought she'd lost her mind. They didn't know the woman who desperately wanted children—she'd kept to herself her infertility and bitterness over Jeff's rejection of her for it. All they saw was an independent woman giving up a successful career as a financial planner on lovely, warm Vancouver

Island to become a mom to six kids in Eastern Ontario—and doing it in winter, no less.

Her own family was much more supportive—smug in fact. If Monica didn't know better, she'd think her mother's hip replacement had been a devious plot to bring her and Luke together.

Devon and Derrick had finished their ceremony and were looking for something else to do. She glanced at her watch. It was almost time for the other children to arrive from school. "Let's get some snacks ready," she called out as she followed them back to the yard.

A grey sedan was parked in the driveway, and a very pregnant young woman was struggling to get out.

"Hello," Monica said, hurrying over to the woman. "Can I help you?"

"No, no, no." The woman sighed heavily as she shimmied around to get her feet on the ground. "Thank you. I can manage. It won't be much longer, thank goodness." When she'd straightened and pushed closed the car door, she turned and smiled.

She appeared to be in her late twenties, with short blonde hair. She was wheezing slightly from the exertion of getting out of the car. Her bulky winter coat looked as if it belonged to a man, and she wore very practical snow boots on her feet. "You must be Monica Stevens," she said. "I'm Lydia Burkholder. I'm with Social Services."

"Oh," Monica said, surprised. "I didn't realize we were due for an inspection. Usually, someone calls first, but no matter. Come on in."

"Oh, no. I'm not here to inspect the daycare," the woman said. "I'm here about Derrick and Devon McMillan."

Monica glanced toward the tire swing. Luke and her mother had convinced her to leave it up and, despite her reservations, she'd agreed. The twins were given very strict guidelines about how they were to use the swing and, fortunately, at this moment they seemed to be following them. Derrick was sedately pushing Devon, but she knew their exuberance could escalate at any moment, and there could be a repeat of the flying incident if she didn't keep an eye on them.

"Of course," Monica said. "Derrick is doing just fine since the fall. There hasn't been any sign of concussion."

"You misunderstand, Ms. Stevens."

"Monica, please."

"Monica." She nodded. "Please call me Lydia. I'm here about the adoption."

"What adoption?" Monica asked. "The twins?"

Lydia expelled a long sigh. "Would you mind if we went inside and sat down? I find it difficult to stand for any length of time."

"No, of course not." She called for the boys to come inside and set them up with a snack in the kitchen while Lydia sat down on the sofa in the front room. She declined Monica's offer of tea but accepted a glass of water.

"Okay, I think you'd better explain the situation to me," Monica said. "Why would you be here about the twin's adoption? Is this some sort of follow-up?"

Lydia placed the glass on the end table and folded her hands across her ample middle. "I understand congratulations are in order. You and the children's father are going to be married, I hear."

"Yes." Monica was surprised by the conversation's change of direction. "Christmas Eve."

"That's pretty quick, isn't it?"

Monica shrugged. "We didn't see any reason to wait."

Lydia sighed.

"Is there a problem with that?" Monica was perplexed.

"It depends on the reason for your marriage," she said and shifted her bulk on the sofa, seeking a more comfortable position. The effort seemed to exhaust her.

A chill swept down Monica. Why would someone from social services be asking about her reason for marrying Luke? "What are you talking about?"

"People get married for all sorts of reasons, don't they?" Lydia paused, waited, but when Monica didn't comment she continued. "I'm not suggesting you're doing anything illegal. However, you should be aware that your marriage will not necessarily guarantee that Mr. McMillan will retain custody of the two boys."

"Wait a second!" Monica leapt to her feet. "Why wouldn't he keep custody of Devon and Derrick. He's their father."

"Not legally. The adoption was never completed. It's my job to review all the information and determine whether or not remaining with Mr. McMillan is in the best interest of the boys."

"He's a great father," Monica said.

"Who already has four children to care for. As I told Mr. McMillan: that would be a big challenge for a two-parent family never mind a single parent with a full-time job."

"You've talked to Luke about this?"

"Of course."

"I don't understand." Monica's head was aching. "He's had the twins since they were infants. Why was the adoption not completed?"

"That's a very good question. The McMillan adoption was among several files I inherited from my predecessor. While I've been able to close the others, this one is more difficult. There are some, shall we say, irregularities."

"How so?" Monica was fascinated by the wave passing under the tight blouse on Lydia's belly. If their current situation wasn't so distressing, she'd ask the woman how it felt to have a life inside of her.

"For starters, there's usually a ton of paperwork associated with international adoptions. But for Devon and Derrick, I have no documentation whatsoever; nothing to indicate where they came from or even when and how they arrived in this country."

"Are you suggesting Luke's done something wrong?"

Lydia shook her head. "Not necessarily. I'm just trying to get this file closed before my maternity leave. I don't want my replacement to have to face the same mess I had coming into this office."

Monica glanced at the woman. She had to be due very soon. "So, you'll be making your recommendation shortly?"

"As I've explained to Mr. McMillan, I need to get this wrapped up before the new year."

Luke wanted them married by Christmas—a week before her deadline.

"Your purpose in coming here today is what, exactly?" Monica asked.

"To meet you, of course. To try to gauge what sort of environment your marriage will create for the children—"

The cold chill of anxiety returned. "The other children? Their adoptions?"

"Are not in jeopardy," Lydia said quickly. "They have all been officially completed and we have no reason to question their validity or the quality of care being provided by their father."

"But not Derrick and Devon?"

"I'm afraid they are more problematic."

"So, what you're really saying is you think our marriage is nothing more than an attempt to get you to recommend that the adoption proceed." Monica could feel the blood drain from her face and her stomach felt as if it had plunged to the floor. *Is this really happening?*

"I am concerned that Mr. McMillan may have misinterpreted my comments to believe that is the case. You have to admit, your marriage is very sudden. How long have you known each other? A month? Two? I wouldn't be doing my job if I didn't investigate every aspect of this case."

The thundering on the front porch heralded the arrival of the older children from school. Monica dutifully introduced them to Lydia, and then they all went into the kitchen to join Devon and Derrick for snacks. When they were finished, Lydia said goodbye to the children and Monica walked her to her car.

"You're very good with them," Lydia said. "But then, I wouldn't have expected otherwise. Both you and your mother have excellent reputations as childcare providers."

"You just don't think I would make a good mother," Monica said.

"On the contrary, I think you'd make an excellent mother. I can see how much you care for those kids. I'm just not convinced about the wife part. Marriage can be tough at the best of times. If your motive for marrying Mr. McMillan is to keep his family together, I wonder if it will be enough to sustain you through the rough patches."

MONICA HELD herself together long enough to watch the sedan turn onto the road and disappear. Her motive for marrying Luke had nothing to do with keeping the family together. She loved him, but did he feel the same way?

She closed her eyes and allowed the tears to flow down her cheeks. She gasped as great sobs of despair wracked her body. It couldn't be true. She replayed their time together. Luke had never actually said he loved her. He'd said he was crazy about her. He'd said he couldn't stop thinking about her. He'd said he wanted to spend his life with her. But had he said he loved her? No, never.

Was he no different from her ex-husband? Jeff had only wanted her as a vessel to bear his children. Did Luke want her solely as a mother for his? What was wrong with her that a man couldn't want her for herself?

"Monica?"

She hastily wiped away the tears and turned toward Kate, standing on the porch. "Yes, sweetie?" Her voice was raspy.

"I need some help with my math homework. Can you come in now that your friend has gone?"

She took a deep breath and forced a smile. "I'll be right there." She watched Kate go back into the house and bent to pick up a fistful of snow. She pressed it against her eyes, hoping the cold would reduce some of the puffiness.

She was numb. Somehow, she was going to have to get through the next few hours with the kids—and seeing Luke. She wouldn't ask them to stay for dinner tonight. She'd plead a headache to get rid of them and then, when she was alone and could think more clearly, she'd figure out what to do.

EIGHT

Monica shivered as she stood on the stoop to Luke's colonial-style home. She was drenched from the cold rain but hadn't summoned the courage to announce her presence. The prediction that falling temperatures would create icy conditions later in the day had been enough to keep the school buses off the roads. Luke had opted to stay home with his children, telling her to rest and recover from her headache.

If only it were that simple.

Unable to sleep, she'd replayed every conversation she'd had with Luke against the background of Lydia Burkholder's visit. It would be bad enough if he was marrying her solely to save his family, but what if there was something nefarious about the adoption of Devon and Derrick? He'd said they were from Eurasia but seemed to gloss over the details of how he'd come to bring them home.

And she'd thought the details of how he came to adopt his children didn't matter.

She sneezed. *This is stupid.* She'd catch pneumonia if she stood out here much longer. The only way she was going to know the truth was to talk to him. She lifted the brass knocker and allowed it to fall heavily against the wooden door.

She caught her breath when Luke appeared. She'd never seen him dressed so casually before, and he looked incredibly sexy in an old tee-shirt, well-worn jeans, and bare feet. The day-old reddish stubble on his face only added to the sense of intimacy. He was holding a steaming mug of coffee, which he quickly put down on a side-table so he could pull her into the house and into his arms.

"Monica, what are you doing out in the rain? You're soaking wet. Come in. Warm up."

For a few precious seconds, she allowed her head to rest against his chest while she closed her eyes. *Please, let it not be true.*

He bent to kiss her, but she turned her face and stepped away. If she allowed him to kiss her, she was afraid she wouldn't be able to go through with it.

"Let me take your coat and get you some dry clothes."

After shrugging out of the sopping jacket, she handed it to him to hang on a hook. While he jogged upstairs to get her a warm shirt, she listened to the drip, drip, drip of water droplets falling from her jacket onto the rubber mat below.

"Here you are," he said, handing her a sweatshirt. "You can change in the washroom if you'd like."

Monica stepped into the hallway and looked around at the homey collection of photographs and children's art tacked up on the walls. It was odd she'd never been in Luke's home before. She was supposed to marry him in a few weeks and, presumably, this was where they'd live. "Where are the children?"

"I put on a movie for them. I can stop it. They'd love to see you."

"No, that's okay. Maybe later."

After changing into the sweatshirt, she wandered into the kitchen. Luke handed her a mug of coffee. "Are you feeling better?" he asked. "You look tired."

"I didn't sleep very well last night." She stiffened as he came behind her and began to massage her shoulders. "Please stop."

He moved to stand in front of her. "Is something wrong? It's not like you to keep quiet if something's bugging you."

"I had a visitor yesterday. Lydia Burkholder from Social Services."

"Ah." He nodded as if he finally understood what was going on. "Let's sit down, okay?"

She rounded the table and took the seat across from his. She wanted to see him but needed to be far enough away that he couldn't touch her. She couldn't think straight when he touched her.

"Why didn't you tell me you hadn't formally adopted Devon and Derrick?" She kept her tone at a whisper in case the children were nearby.

"It's okay, they're upstairs."They can't hear us, and we'll hear them if they come down." He sighed heavily. "You're right. I should have told you. But there's nothing nefarious or illegal going on. The simple truth is I just forgot to deal with it."

"How do you just forget that you haven't adopted your sons?" She was incredulous.

"It was a complicated adoption. We were in the middle of it when Beth died. All my attention was focused on helping my kids get through that. I always intended to get back to the adoption. I just hadn't done it yet."

It didn't make sense. He'd said he brought the twins home as babies and his wife had died a few years ago. They'd have had the twins for almost two years before her death. "Why isn't there any documentation about where they came from or how they came to Canada?"

"There is documentation. It's just caught up in a jurisdictional quagmire," he said.

Convenient.

"It's a time and place I try not to think about." His eyes clouded and his mouth was set in a firm line. "The aid agency Beth and I worked with asked me to go to Eurasia for one last mission. It was a major screw up right from the start." He shuddered. "Bad intelligence all 'round."

His voice had become rough. "I'd been in a village inland for only a few days when we received word that insurgents were in the area and they were heading our way. But the news was old. There wasn't time to do a proper evacuation. I was trying to help the nuns organize the orphans to go hide in the mountains, but there were these two babies..."

"Derrick and Devon."

Luke nodded. "There was no way the nuns could take care of them away from the village and we knew—or at least we were pretty sure—that the insurgents weren't interested in harming Westerners. Sister Beatrice thrust the boys into my arms and begged me to take them to Canada, to give them a good life."

"Did they get away? The nuns and the children?" She

felt compelled to ask even though she was afraid she already knew the answer.

His face had gone grey. "No. I managed to hide the boys so when the insurgents came into the village, I was the only one they found there. They didn't bother with me—too political, I guess. They took off right away and chased the others into the mountains where they massacred them all. It was likely just my conscience, but I swear I could hear their screams as I drove away. I still hear them some nights."

Tears stung her eyes, and she reached across the table to clasp Luke's hand. "I'm so sorry."

He looked down at their hands and smiled weakly. "I brought the boys home on an emergency military transport. I knew Beth would welcome them, and she did. Before we could adopt them, however, we had to ensure they really were orphans and not just separated from their families. It was so chaotic over there."

"That's what took all the time," she said, understanding.

"Yeah. The aid agency, foreign affairs, a bunch of other organizations were involved. It was just before Beth's aneurism that we got the okay to proceed." He looked up. "I have no idea which of these agencies has the documentation Ms. Burkholder is looking for, but I have no doubt it exists."

She closed her eyes and breathed a sigh of relief. Luke was an honourable man. But the missing documentation was only one of Lydia Burkholder's concerns with the adoption. There was also their marriage. She knew she shouldn't allow the woman to play to her fears, but she needed to know the truth.

"She also thinks you're marrying me so the twins will have both a mother and father."

"Is that a bad thing?" He looked surprised. "Isn't that best for every child?"

Monica pulled her hands back. "Just because a family doesn't have two parents doesn't mean it's bad for the kids. Look at my family. My dad died when Cathy and I were young, and Mom did just fine. We all know families with a mother and father that are not happy."

"True, but that's not us. Look how well we get along. I'm crazy about you. The kids love you."

"The kids love me, but do you?"

"What?" Confusion clouded his face.

"It's a different kind of love, between a man and a woman. I want to know if you feel that for me." Monica could feel her dreams slipping away when he didn't immediately respond, but she strengthened her resolve and took a leap of faith. "I feel it for you. I love you, Luke. I'm *in love* with you."

Confusion had changed to panic, and he stared back at her as if she were speaking a foreign language.

The crushing pain in her chest was something she never thought she'd experience again—she hadn't believed she was capable of feeling that kind of hurt, that kind of betrayal any more. But she had her answer. And as her heart broke into a million pieces, a wave of inevitability washed over her. Maybe tomorrow she'd rant and rave at the unfairness of it all like she'd done when her marriage to Jeff had ended, but for now, she wasn't angry. She was just sad. Very sad for what she'd almost had and lost—again.

She twisted the diamond ring off her finger, placed it on the table between them, and rose to leave. "I'm sorry."

Monica hoped the end of their engagement wouldn't jeopardize Luke's chances to adopt Derrick and Devon. She'd talk to Lydia, try to convince her that keeping the McMillans together was the right thing to do. But regardless of what happened, she couldn't marry someone who didn't want her for herself. She'd been down that road before and, despite his contention that they were good together, it would inevitably lead to heartbreak.

She grabbed her jacket from the hook and wrapped it around her shoulders, bracing herself to return out into the freezing rain. As she closed the door, she could hear him calling her name, asking her to wait. But she couldn't go back.

NINE

"Is Monica here, Daddy?" Devon's face appeared at the top of the stairs, immediately joined by Derrick and Luke's other children.

"No, she just stopped in for a quick moment. She's gone now." Luke tried to steel himself against the looks of disappointment on their faces as they returned to the movie. It would be worse when they found out Monica wasn't going to marry him and join their family.

He winced when he remembered her expression when he couldn't say what she wanted to hear. *Way to go, man. Now you've gone and screwed up everyone's life!*

He still wasn't quite sure what had happened. He'd never lied to her about his feelings; he'd just never thought about whether or not he was *in love* with her.

Jeez, they weren't kids. Love. In love. What did it matter what the words were? They made a perfect team. They both loved the kids and worked well together. And in bed...well, definitely no complaints there. He hadn't been lying when he'd told her he wanted to marry quickly so they could spend their nights together.

After Beth, he never thought he'd find someone who would fill his emptiness—someone he'd want to spend the rest of his life with.

Sure, it was also good for the adoption, but who said the same end couldn't serve a dual purpose?

He'd never intended to hurt her. Hell, he never wanted to see that pained look on her face again. In fact, if anyone else had put it there, he'd have pummelled the bastard.

She was special. They really could have a wonderful life together. He wanted to give her that life—give her everything she'd always wanted but had never been able to have. Three little words were all that was standing between them. And yet, he knew it wasn't simply the words; it was the feeling behind them.

What was wrong with him?

He fingered the engagement ring he'd stuck in his pocket. Maybe he could talk to her again? Get her to change her mind? At the very least he needed to make sure she was okay and apologize for hurting her.

After arranging for Stephanie and Jennifer to look after the children, Luke set off for Monica's home. The rain had turned to freezing rain and the road was slick with a thin layer of ice. He dropped his speed and resisted using the brakes whenever possible, and yet he almost slid off the road twice.

In his mind, he rehearsed what he wanted to say to her, vacillating between convincing her to marry him despite her doubts and simply apologizing for hurting her. He didn't want to lose her, but he wanted to do the right thing...for her.

A flash of orange appeared as he rounded a corner and he slammed on his brakes, sending his van into a spin that ended with him on the other shoulder facing the opposite direction. Thank goodness there hadn't been another car coming. He cut the engine and skated across the road to where an orange-coloured sub-compact was lying on its side in a ditch.

"Monica!"

Crap, there was a lot of blood. Her face was covered with it, and she wasn't moving. Her breathing was laboured, but at least she was breathing. He pulled out his cell phone and dialled 9-1-1. "Hurry," he urged the operator.

"Monica, honey, you're going to be okay. Help's coming." He gingerly brushed her hair from her face. Where had all the blood come from?

It seemed like forever before the paramedics arrived. She still hadn't regained consciousness when he watched them load her into the ambulance. Following her to the hospital was like reliving the nightmare of Beth's aneurism.

Monica had to be okay. Surely, fate wouldn't be so cruel as to take away the two women he loved.

MONICA'S FACE WAS BANDAGED, and she was propped up on a cot in an emergency room cubicle when Luke was finally allowed to see her. She seemed surprised he was there. "I heard someone was here to get me. I assumed it was Cathy," she said.

"I told Cathy I'd bring you home. There's no point

both of us driving on these roads," he said. "Are you okay?" She looked small and frail, but at least she was alive.

"It's just a broken nose from the airbag." She shrugged nonchalantly and then cocked her head to one side and grinned. "I asked them if they could give me a nose job while they were at it, but they said my out-of-province insurance wouldn't cover it."

He knew she was trying to lighten the mood, but he'd been so worried about her he couldn't find the humour in her words. "You don't need a nose job, Monica. You're perfect just the way you are."

Her eyes widened in surprise and then narrowed. "Are *you* okay? You don't look well. Maybe you should sit down."

His body was shaking with the relief of knowing that she was going to be all right. He sank into the chair beside her cot. "I was so afraid when I saw your car...and then there was so much blood..." He heaved a shuddering breath. "I thought I'd lost you. I can't lose you..."

"Luke—" She said his name quietly, but there was so much anguish in her voice that he felt his heart constrict at his own selfishness.

"No," he interrupted her. "Let me say something, first." He gazed into the beautiful hazel eyes staring out from the bandages that masked half her face. There was some bruising around her chin. Only her mouth seemed unaffected by the accident, and he yearned to taste her lips—to hold her, to make love to her, to demonstrate with his body what his words lacked. "Earlier you asked me if I loved you, and I didn't answer."

"That was an answer. Don't feel sorry for me because of a broken nose. I'll be fine. Really."

"I don't feel sorry for you," he said. "I feel sorry for me. I feel sorry because I think my self-focus may have lost me the woman I love. I couldn't tell you I loved you before because I'd only been thinking about us in terms of how great we are together and how fantastic it was that everything was going to work out for us—you'd get the family you've always wanted, and I'd get to keep mine together. It seemed a win-win for everyone."

"This isn't one of your development projects to be negotiated to a satisfactory conclusion," she snapped.

"You're right. This is the most important deal of my life, and it has nothing to do with you becoming a mother to my children or me being able to adopt Devon and Derrick. It has to do with you and me. I don't want to live my life without you. That became crystal clear when I saw your car in the ditch and found you unconscious inside. The kids didn't even enter my mind at that point. It was just me selfishly praying for you to be all right so I can tell you how much I love you and ask you to forgive me for making you doubt how precious you are to me."

She closed her eyes, and he watched a small tear trail down her bandaged cheek. He reached out to wipe it away, but stopped himself, afraid his touch, no matter how tender, would inflict pain. He let his hand drop to his lap and lowered his head. Maybe he was too late.

"I forgive you."

It was spoken so softly he wasn't sure he'd heard anything. "What?" He raised his head to look at her.

She opened her eyes and glared at him. "I said I forgive you," she said, louder this time and sounding slightly annoyed. "I just wish it hadn't taken a damaged rental car and a broken nose for you to say it."

Luke whooped with joy and leapt to his feet. "Marry me," he said, falling to his knees beside her cot. He fumbled in his pocket until he found her ring and held it up to her. "It doesn't have to be right away. We can wait as long as you want, but just say you'll be my wife."

She held her hand out for him to place the diamond ring on her finger. "I don't see the point in waiting. Everything's already set for Christmas Eve."

He stood up, kissed the ring on her hand, and then bent down and brushed his mouth against her beautiful lips. He forced himself to keep the kiss gentle, curbing his growing desire so as not to aggravate her injuries.

When he finally raised his head, he realized they'd attracted an audience. A nurse had pulled back the curtain and several doctors stood at the foot of Monica's cot. The patient across the room was also gawking at them.

"She said 'yes'," he said, and then took a deep bow as the room erupted with applause.

Monica was rolling her eyes at his antics, but her wide grin told him she was happy. Luke pledged to find a way to put that look on her face every day for the rest of their lives.

TEN

Monica couldn't have asked for a more perfect day for her wedding. There had been a light dusting of snow the night before, but the morning had dawned clear and crisp. As she descended the stairs of her mother's house and paused on the threshold to the front room, she was overwhelmed by the love she felt from her family as they turned toward her.

Terry had returned home the week previous and had thrown herself into wedding preparation mode, enlisting the children's help in creating all sorts of decorations and delicacies. With Christmas being the following day, the house was festooned in colours of red, white, and gold with both giant paper snowflakes and giant paper peonies hanging from the ceiling. A beautiful white spruce tree sat in the corner, its tiny blinking lights highlighting handcrafted ornaments from her youth. A similar tree sat in Luke's living room and showcased his children's handiwork.

Cathy beamed at Monica while Phil gave her a wink. Beside them, Stephanie and Jennifer were dabbing their eyes—teenage girls! While they were happy their favourite aunt was going to be staying in town and looked forward to more shopping expeditions, the girls admitted they were disappointed to see the end of their annual Vancouver Island vacation. She turned away quickly, afraid the overly emotional girls would cause her own eyes to tear up.

Devon and Derrick waved as she passed them. They were dressed in nice pants and dress shirts, while their more sedate sisters wore lovely floral dresses. Stephanie and Jennifer had been in charge of outfitting the children and they'd done a wonderful job. Michael wore a dark suit with a red tie. His expression was intense as she approached. He'd been given responsibility for the wedding rings, and he took his role very seriously.

But it was Luke who stole her breath away. When she turned her gaze to him, she couldn't look away. His eyes roamed the length of her body, appreciating the way the simple ivory gown clung to her breasts, waist, and hips before flowing down to the floor. He smiled a slow, sexy smile as he reached out to take her hand, and she had no doubt that he was thinking about their wedding night. She felt a warm flush creep up her face.

While the minister spoke, their family formed a semi-circle around Monica and Luke. He hadn't even finished telling the groom he could kiss his bride, when she was caught up in a passionate embrace that left her dazed and breathless, and wondering if it would be considered rude were they to make an early exit from the festivities.

The twins couldn't wait to get out of their dress-up clothes and go outside to check on the geese. They were worried about Anna; despite the nice weather, she hadn't come out of the bird barn for several days. Michael, Kate, Lucy, and Ophelia followed. Stephanie and Jennifer thought they'd stay with the adults, but when they were informed they wouldn't be allowed any of the champagne Phil had just poured, they grumbled about the unfairness of the world and joined the children outside.

Phil raised a toast to welcome Luke to the family just as a loud knock sounded on the front door.

"Are you expecting someone?" Monica asked her mother as she placed her glass down on a table to go answer it.

"Oh, dear, I'm interrupting," Lydia Burkholder said when she saw Monica's wedding gown.

The elation Monica had been feeling evaporated.

"I'm looking for Mr. McMillan. I went to his home, but he wasn't there. I took a chance that he might be here."

She knew Lydia wanted to complete her recommendation concerning the adoption of Devon and Derrick by year's end, but Luke hadn't mentioned anything about it in weeks, and she hadn't asked. Was that why she was here now?

"Monica? Is everything..." Luke came into the foyer and stopped. "Ms. Burkholder," he said dumbly.

"I'm so sorry to intrude," she said, "but I needed to speak with you."

"Do you want to come in?" Monica didn't want to invite the woman in—she was dreading what news she might bring—however, Lydia was very pregnant, and it just seemed wrong to force her to stand outside on the front step.

"No, thank you. I'll be quick."

Luke reached for Monica's hand. "I assume you're here to tell us your recommendation concerning the boys."

"Yes, I am."

Did Lydia have to look so serious? Monica closed her eyes and said a silent prayer. *Please, don't take Devon and Derrick away from us. Not today. Not ever.*

"I was finally able to locate the documents you mentioned, Mr. McMillan. I'm used to bureaucratic red tape, but let me tell you, I've never experienced an administrative nightmare quite like that before."

Just get to it!

Or maybe she didn't want her to. After all, the longer Lydia delayed, the longer Monica was Devon and Derrick's mother. Could she and Luke appeal if they didn't like the recommendation?

Luke stood stone-still, barely breathing. *This must be killing him.* She squeezed his hand. Regardless of the outcome, they'd get through this. She could help him if it didn't go their way. She knew what it was like to lose a hoped-for child. This wasn't quite the same, of course. Her children had only been in her dreams while Derrick and Devon were real and loving and... She stifled a sob.

"Oh, my goodness," Lydia said, noting her distress. "I should have just come out and said it right away rather than have you standing here thinking the worst. How thoughtless of me. I'm recommending the adoption proceed."

Monica and Luke turned to each other, suddenly dizzy

with relief. They embraced and then pulled Lydia into their hug.

"Thank you." Luke's voice was hoarse, and tears were running down his face. Hers, too, Monica realized.

"Daddy, Mommy, you have to come and see!" Devon raced across the yard toward them.

Monica's heart stopped. He'd called her "Mommy"— words she never thought she'd hear. Someone she never thought she'd be. She glanced at Luke. From his grin he'd heard it, too.

"Whoa, there," Luke said, swinging Devon up into his arms and hugging him as if he'd never let him go.

"It's Anna," Devon said, wiggling down to the ground. "She's going to be a mommy."

"Maybe in the spring," Monica said. She'd been reading up on geese.

"C'mon." Devon pulled both Monica and Luke down the steps toward the bird barn. "You, too, lady," he called over his shoulder to Lydia.

The barn was dimly lit, but warm, which was good because her wedding gown was hardly suitable outdoor attire. Luke had given her his suit jacket and that had cut the chill somewhat.

"Over here," Derrick called excitedly.

The crowd of children parted when the adults approached.

Monica gazed down at the motley-coloured goose sitting in her nest. The bird gazed back, patiently. Kristoff wandered around, squawking occasionally. He wasn't pleased that so many people had invaded the small barn.

"She's sitting on eggs," Derrick said.

Monica shook her head. "That's highly unlikely this time of year," she said gently.

"No, it's true. I think I saw one when she shifted," Jennifer said.

"I can make her move," Devon said, pushing between the adults. "C'mon Anna." He bent down and rubbed the goose's head, then nudged her to her feet.

Monica stared in disbelief at the six white goose eggs lying in the nest. "That's not supposed to happen," she whispered.

"It's a miracle," Devon said, allowing the goose to settle on her nest again.

"A Christmas miracle," Lydia said, smiling.

"That's the second Christmas miracle we've had today," Luke said, ruffling the heads of his two youngest sons.

"No," Monica said, wrapping her arms around her new husband. "It's the third."

Luke brought his mouth down onto hers in a long, slow kiss that conveyed all the love and expectation for a future Monica had given up hope of ever having.

Lover. Wife. Mother.

It truly was a Christmas miracle.

What's next in the **Seasons of Love** series? Let's take a trip to Sedona, Arizona.

Teacher Lori Tait has always wanted a family, but now she's passing 40, she's pretty much decided all the good men are taken. Instead, she devotes herself to her students, particularly one little girl whose struggle with math seems inconsistent with an otherwise brilliant and artistic mind.

Mark Wilder hadn't planned to become a father, but when a fling resulted in his daughter, Grace, he whole-heartedly embraced the role. Raised in a family of boys, what does he know about women and girls? Once he learns of Grace's inability to comprehend basic math, he welcomes the role of tutor as a way to connect with his daughter; the opportunity to spend time with her sexy teacher is an added bonus.

When Lori cracks the mystery of Grace's problem, Mark's world is thrown into turmoil; he's the last person who can help his daughter. He pushes everyone away, confirming Lori's theory about men. Grace, however, has other plans. Using her new-found understanding of math, she sets out to prove to her father and teacher that, together, they add up to the perfect match.

Pre-order *The Color of You* today and prepare for a romantic Valentine's day among the beautiful red rock mountains of Sedona. (Available February 10, 2026)

IF YOU ENJOYED *Six Geese for Monica*, please let your friends know so they can experience Monica and Luke's romance as well. If you leave a review on your favourite retailer, book site, or your own blog, I'd love to read it. Email me the link at brenda@brendagayle.com.

You can stay up-to-date on upcoming releases, giveaways, sales and all sorts of shenanigans by joining my newsletter, *The Gayle Gazette.*
Go to brendagayle.com to sign up.

ARE you looking for something a little different? How about a romantic suspense?

A burned-out executive spices things up with Santa Fe's celebrated cowboy chef unaware that a secret in her past could send their future up in smoke.

Child advocate Nora Cross doesn't have time for the private cooking lessons her sister won from a charity auction, especially when it comes to the hunk giving the lessons. Hunter Graham may be Santa Fe's most popular chef-restauranteur, but he's also the most arrogant man Nora has ever met. He has the nerve to tell her she's too uptight and doesn't know how to relax and have fun...so why can't she get him off her mind?

After a stellar debut in New York City, Hunter's back in Santa Fe to open a new restaurant. He lives a charmed life, and he knows it. He isn't interested in a workaholic woman who's glued to her smartphone, so why is he trying to convince Nora to relax and enjoy life—with him?

When Nora's apartment and office are ransacked, Hunter comes to her rescue, surprised to find himself playing knight-in-shining-armor. But when he discovers

Nora is no random target, Hunter realizes he'll do anything to keep her safe.

Get The Hungry Heart to add some sizzle to your day!

The Hungry Heart is the first book in the Heart's Desire Series. Available exclusively on Amazon.

What would you risk for your heart's desire?

ABOUT BRENDA GAYLE

I've been a writer all my life but returned to my love of fiction after more than 20 years in the world of corporate communications—although some might argue there is plenty of opportunity for fiction-writing there, too. A fan of many genres, I find it hard to stay within the publishing industry's prescribed boxes. Whether it's historical mystery, romantic suspense, or women's fiction, my greatest joy is creating deeply emotional books with memorable characters and compelling stories.

Connect with me on my website at BrendaGayle.com & sign up for *The Gayle Gazette,* my newsletter, to keep up-to-date on new releases, exclusive access to special features, giveaways, and all sorts of shenanigans

Until next time...

f facebook.com/brendagaylebooks

ALSO BY BRENDA GAYLE

SEASONS OF LOVE

Twice & Forever - Autumn

Six Geese for Monica - Winter

The Color of You - Spring

The Parent Trip - Summer (coming May 2026)

Operation Soft Landing

(a military romantic suspense, coming Winter 2025/26)

HEART'S DESIRE ROMANTIC SUSPENSE

The Hungry Heart

The Doubting Heart

The Forsaken Heart